Hello Kitty's Garden Party

By Elizabeth Bennett
Illustrated by Sachiho Hino

SCHOLASTIC INC.

New York   Toronto   London   Auckland   Sydney
Mexico City   New Delhi   Hong Kong   Buenos Aires

No part of this publication may be reproduced, stored in a retrieval system, or transmitted in any form or by any means, electronic, mechanical, photocopying, recording, or otherwise, without written permission of the publisher. For information regarding permission, write to SANRIO, INC., 990 West 190th Street, Suite 220, Torrance, CA 90502.

ISBN-13: 978-0-439-87137-2

ISBN-10: 0-439-87137-9

Text and illustrations © 2007 SANRIO CO., LTD. USED UNDER LICENSE.

Character © 1976 SANRIO CO., LTD. USED UNDER LICENSE.

12 11 10 9 8 7 6 5 4 3   9 10 11 12/0

Printed in the U.S.A.

First printing, March 2007

 looks out the 🪟.

The ☀️ is shining. 🐦🐦 are singing.

It is spring!

🐱 loves spring.

Every spring she helps 🐱 plant

a big 🌷.

But this year is different.

🐱 has broken her 🦵.

Her 🦵 is in a 🩹 and she can't

work in the 🌼.

🐱 is sad that she won't have

a 🌼 this year.

🐱 tells 🐱, "I will plant the

🌼 all by myself!"

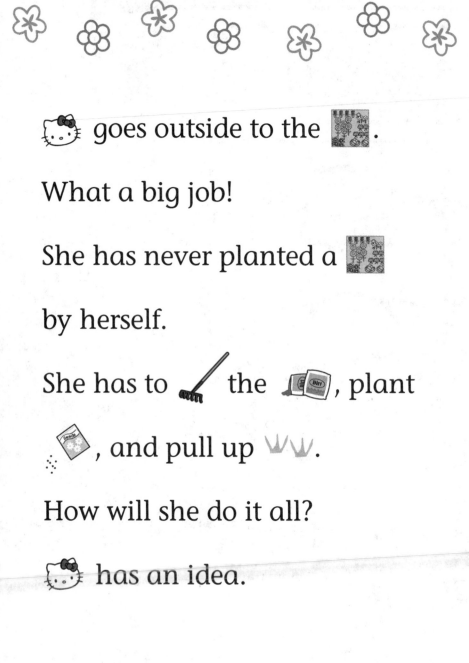

goes outside to the .

What a big job!

She has never planted a

by herself.

She has to the , plant

, and pull up .

How will she do it all?

has an idea.

She goes inside to call .

Next  calls .

"Can you bring a  ?"

she asks him.

"I will bring a  and  !"

 answers.

's friends will help her plant

the .

 is going to help, too!

The next day 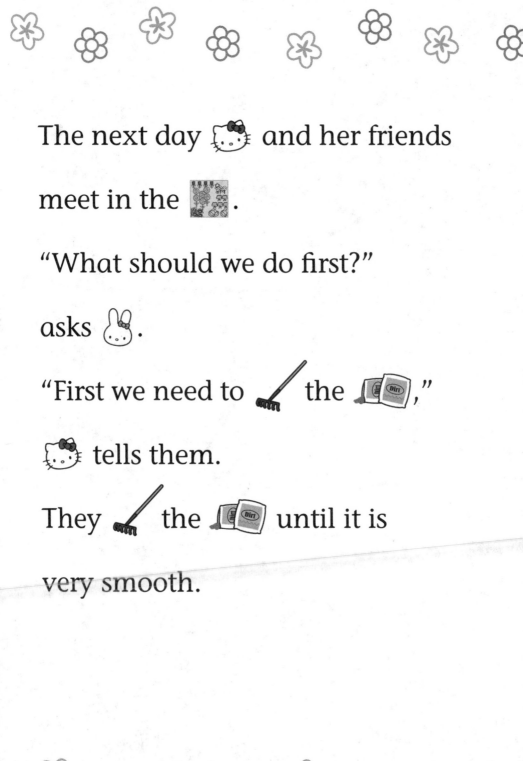 and her friends

meet in the 🌸 .

"What should we do first?"

asks 🐰 .

"First we need to 🌾 the 📖 Dirt ,"

🐱 tells them.

They 🌾 the 📖 Dirt until it is

very smooth.

Now it is time to plant the .

Oh, no!

 does not have any .

"We can go to the  to buy

," she tells her friends.

 and her friends enjoy the spring

breeze as they walk to the .

The 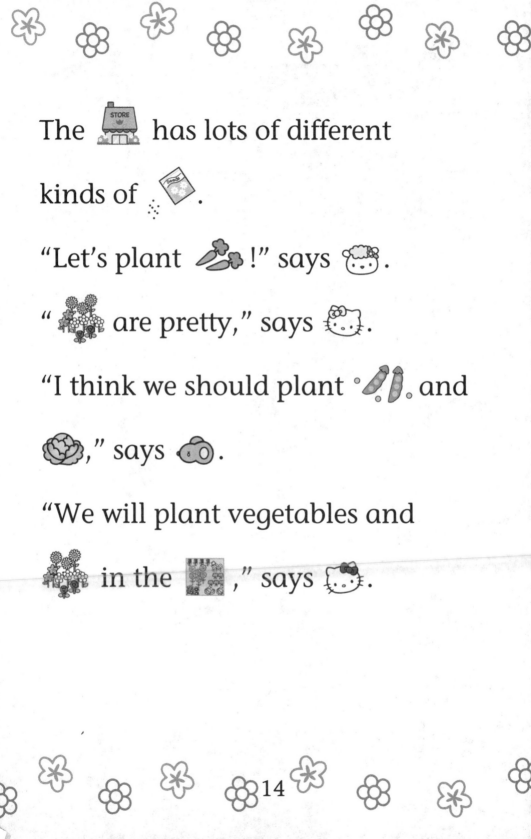 has lots of different

kinds of .

"Let's plant !" says .

" are pretty," says .

"I think we should plant and

," says .

"We will plant vegetables and

in the ," says .

Back at the 🏡 🐱 shows her
friends how to use a 🔨 to dig
small holes for the 🌱.
They plant 🥕, 🫛, and
🥬 on one side of the 🏡.
They plant rows of 🌼 on
the other side.

🐱 comes outside to see the 🏡.
"Plants need lots of water," 🐱 says.
She gives 🐱 her 🫖.

🐱 visits the 🌷 every day.

Sometimes 🐱 comes with her.

Sometimes 🐰 comes with her.

Sometimes she goes by herself.

They water the 🌱 with the 🪣.

They pull up 🌿.

🐱 and her friends take very good care of 🐱's 🌱.

The 🌱 grow into plants.

The 🥕, 🫛, and 🥬 are ready to pick.

Beautiful 🌸 are blooming.

And 🐱's 💪 is all better.

Her 🩹 has come off!

It is time to celebrate!

"Let's have a  party!" says 🐱.

She makes a big salad with the 🥬,

🫛, and 🥕.

🐱 picks lots of 🌸.

🐑 makes 🍿.

"What a pretty 🌸," says 🐱.

🐱 answers, "I did it all by myself –

with a little help from my friends!"

Did you spot all the picture clues in this Hello Kitty book?

Each picture clue is on a flash card. Ask a grown-up to cut out the flash cards. Then try reading the words on the back of the cards. The pictures will be your clue.

Reading is fun with Hello Kitty !

window	Hello Kitty
birds	sun
garden	Grandma

cast

arm

dirt

rake

weeds

seeds

STORE

Joey	Kathy
Mimmy	Fifi
carrots	store

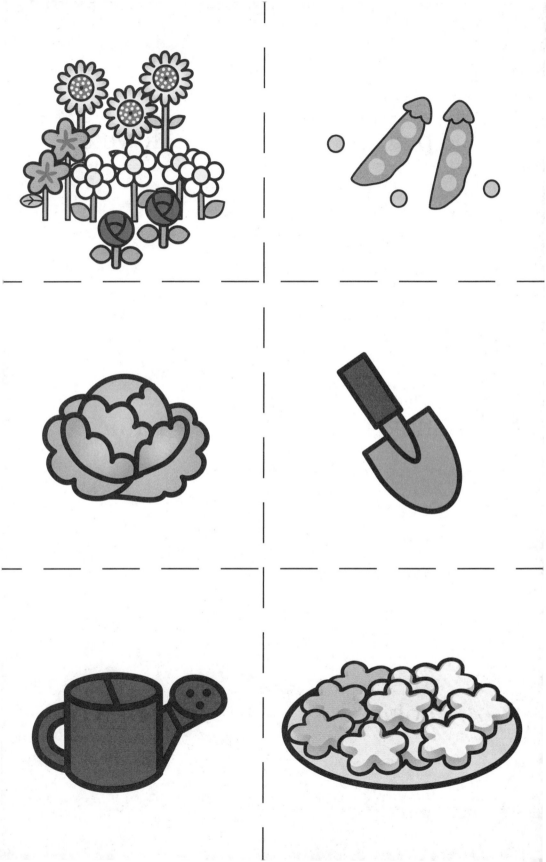

peas	flowers
shovel	lettuce
cookies	watering can